Katie Woo's

✳ Neighborhood ✳

Friends in the Mail

by Fran Manushkin

illustrated by Laura Zarrin

PICTURE WINDOW BOOKS
a capstone imprint

Katie Woo's Neighborhood is published by Picture Window Books,
A Capstone Imprint
1710 Roe Crest Drive
North Mankato, Minnesota 56003
www.capstonepub.com

Text © 2020 Fran Manushkin
Illustrations © 2020 Picture Window Books

All rights reserved. No part of this publication may be reproduced in
whole or in part, or stored in a retrieval system, or transmitted in any
form or by any means, electronic, mechanical, photocopying, recording,
or otherwise, without written permission of the publisher.

Library of Congress Cataloging-in-Publication Data
Names: Manushkin, Fran, author. | Zarrin, Laura, illustrator.
Title: Friends in the mail / Fran Manushkin ; illustrator, Laura Zarrin.
Description: North Mankato, MN : Picture Window Books, [2019] | Series:
    Katie Woo. Katie Woo's neighborhood | "Picture Window Books are
    published by Capstone"—Copyright page. | Summary: On a trip to the
    post office to mail a present to her grandfather, Katie learns all about
    how the mail works.
Identifiers: LCCN 2019007674| ISBN 9781515844587 (hardcover) |
    ISBN 9781515845584 (pbk.) | ISBN 9781515844624 (ebook pdf)
Subjects: LCSH: Woo, Katie (Fictitious character)—Juvenile fiction. |
    Chinese Americans—Juvenile fiction. | Postal service—Juvenile fiction. |
    CYAC: Chinese Americans—Fiction. | Postal service—Fiction.
Classification: LCC PZ7.M3195 Fr 2019 | DDC 813.54 [E]—dc23
LC record available at https://lccn.loc.gov/2019007674

Graphic Designer: Bobbie Nuytten

Printed and bound in the USA.
PA71

Table of Contents

Katie's Neighborhood

Police

Library

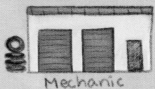

Mechanic

City
Hall

Grocery Store

Post Office

Chapter 1
A Gift for Grandpa

Katie made a scarf for her grandpa's birthday. It took her a long time.

"We should mail it today," said Katie's mom. "Grandpa's birthday is very soon."

"Let's go!" said Katie.

Katie and her mom

began walking to the post

office.

"Hey, Katie," yelled Pedro.

"Look at the soccer stickers

I got in the mail."

"They look cool!" said Katie. "Maybe I'll order some too. But right now we have to mail my grandpa's present."

On the next block, Katie saw Sharon, her mail carrier. Sharon was telling JoJo, "I have something for you."

"Look!" said JoJo. "I wrote a letter to an astronaut, and I got a photo back."

"Great!" said Sharon. "I love bringing happy mail!"

Chapter 2

At the Post Office

Katie and her mom
hurried to the post office.
They saw trucks bringing
in mail and trucks taking
other mail away.

"Hi, Miss Roxie," Katie said to the clerk. "I want to mail this birthday present. I hope it gets there in time."

Miss Roxie smiled. "It will! We deliver in sunny weather and in the rain and the snow."

Just then, Haley O'Hara and her five brothers and sisters came into the post office.

"We are mailing letters to our pen pals," said Haley. "They all live in different cities."

Katie asked Miss Roxie,

"How do you know where

to send each letter?"

"With zip codes," said Miss Roxie. "That helps us sort each letter. Then it will go to the right place."

Lee Gomez
20 First St.
San Jose, CA 95125

"Does the mail always travel in trucks?" asked Haley. "I want to be a truck driver when I grow up."

"No," said Miss Roxie.

"The mail also goes by plane

and sometimes by boat."

Chapter 3

Back Home Again

As Katie and her mom left the post office, Katie waved at a mail truck.

She said, "I hope they take good care of my grandpa's present."

On the way home,
Katie's mom asked, "Have
you ever heard about the
Pony Express?"

"No," said Katie.

Her mother explained,
"A long time ago, mail was
carried from place to place
on horses."

"Wow!" said Katie. "I'd
love to be the rider and
bring birthday presents."

When Katie got home,
she called her grandpa and
said, "I mailed you a present
for your birthday. I hope you
like it."

Katie's gift arrived in time.

Did her grandpa love it?

He did!

Glossary

astronaut (AS-truh-nawt)—someone who travels in space

deliver (di-LIV-ur)—to take something to someone

mail carrier (MAYL KAR-ee-ur)—a person who delivers the mail to a house or office or picks it up from mailboxes

mail clerk (MAYL KLURK)—a person who does general work, such as selling stamps or sorting mail, at a post office

Pony Express (POH-nee ek-SPRESS)—a mail service in which a series of riders carried the mail on horseback from Missouri to California. Pony Express service began in April 1860 and ended in October 1861.

post office (POHST OFF-iss)—the place people go to buy stamps and to send letters and packages

Katie's Questions

1. What traits or skills does a mail carrier need? Would you like to be a mail carrier? Why or why not?

2. Compare Sharon the mail carrier's job with Roxie the mail clerk's job. How are they the same? How are they different?

3. Think about your local post office, or better yet, take a trip there. Then make a list of at least five words or phrases to describe your post office.

4. If you could write a letter to anyone, who would you write to? Now write that letter, and mail it if you can.

5. If you were in charge of designing a stamp, what would you put on it? Now draw your idea!

Katie Interviews Mail Carrier Sharon

Katie: Hi, Sharon! Thanks for talking to me about your job as a mail carrier.

Sharon: I'm happy to, Katie. I just love delivering mail!

Katie: What is your favorite part of your job?

Sharon: I like being outside in the fresh air. When I'm walking my route, sometimes I see kids out playing, and they always say hello. I'm even friends with some of the dogs on my route. I love giving them treats!

Katie: Do mail carriers take special classes to become a carrier?

Sharon: You have to graduate from high school. Then you must pass a special test with the post office. And before you get your own route, you will train with an experienced mail carrier.

Katie: Is the mail pack really heavy?

Sharon: I fill it with up to 35 pounds of mail, which sounds like a lot. But it keeps me strong. Some carriers have bigger loads that they push in a special cart. That can be tricky in the winter!

Katie: That's right—you have to deliver mail in all sorts of weather. Does some weather make your job harder?

Sharon: Winter can be very cold, but I wear lots of layers of clothes and heavy boots. I like my summer uniform more! I get to wear shorts and a cap in the summer.

About the Author

Fran Manushkin is the author of Katie Woo, the highly acclaimed, fan-favorite early reader series, as well as the popular Pedro series. Her other books include *Happy in Our Skin, Baby, Come Out!* and the best-selling board books *Big Girl Panties* and *Big Boy Underpants*. There is a real Katie Woo: Fran's great-niece, who doesn't get into trouble like the Katie in the books. Fran lives in New York City, three blocks from Central Park, where she can often be found bird-watching and daydreaming. She writes at her dining room table, without the help of her two naughty cats, Chaim and Goldy.

About the Illustrator

Laura Zarrin spent her early childhood in the St. Louis, Missouri, area. There she explored creeks, woods, and attic closets, climbed trees, and dug for artifacts in the backyard, all in preparation for her future career as an archeologist. She never became one, however, because she realized she's much happier drawing in the comfort of her own home while watching TV. When she was twelve, her family moved to the Silicon Valley in California, where she still resides with her very logical husband and teen sons, and their illogical dog, Cody.